Please return / renew by date shown.
You can renew it at:
norlink.norfolk.gov.uk
or by telephone: 0344 800 8006
Please have your library card & PIN ready

KT-474-303

NORFOLK LIBRARY
AND INFORMATION SERVICE

NORFOLK ITEM

17 **Pig** gets Angry

18 **Pig**'s Season's Finale   ... and more!

PIG Gets Angry
by Barbara Catchpole
Illustrated by Dynamo

Published by Ransom Publishing Ltd.
Unit 7, Brocklands Farm, West Meon, Hampshire
GU32 1JN, UK
www.ransom.co.uk

ISBN   978 178127 539 9
First published in 2015

Gets

Angry

Barbara Catchpole

Illustrated by Dynamo

Ransom

Teachers behaving badly

At four o'clock on Monday I was standing in front of a class, trying to teach a load of idiots about fractions.

The idiots were teachers.

The teachers were idiots. They were mucking about.

Mr Jones was picking his nose! He held his other hand up to hide it, but I knew what he was doing. I'm an

expert at picking your nose in class without being seen.

Miss Hardcastle and Mr Strange were whispering and giggling. I couldn't find the remote for the whiteboard – then I saw the dinner lady putting it in her pocket.

Mr Lamb was writing on the desk and Miss

Joseph was going to flick a rubber band at the back of Mr Rainbow's head. It hit my nose instead.

I wasn't crying, of course, but it made my eyes water.

They were all being horrible! And there really was a bad smell in the classroom. Who had done that? I didn't think teachers ever, well, you know ...

I'll tell you how I got in this mess.

Sunday

'Piiiiig! Get in here!'

Mum was in the kitchen.

'Wanna talk to you, my little wombat!'

Now Mum only ever wants to talk to me for one of three reasons.

1. I had done something I shouldn't have done

I had a good think. What had I done?

I hadn't put Suki's keys in her shoes for ages, or a slug in her bed, or her keys in her bed and a slug in her shoe.

I knew! I had dropped her strawberry lip gloss down the toilet. I was just licking it to see if it was like a strawberry sweet.

Loads of things get dropped down the toilet in our house anyway. Suki dropped her

9

false eyelash in there and I thought it was an insect with loads of legs and I weed on it.

When we were looking after Mrs Zielinski's goldfish and it died (she'd only been away an hour) Mum flushed it down the loo and bought another one that looked exactly the same.

Mum said it's cruel for a fish to live in a chip shop anyway. She said it had to watch all its cousins being eaten!

Then one Christmas my grand pop dropped his teeth down the loo.

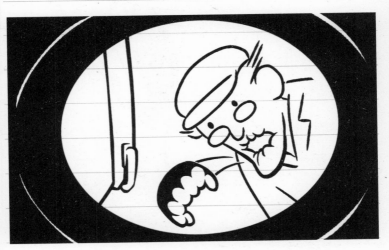

Dad fished them out with Mum's cooking tools and Mum went spare.

(Grand pop dropped his false teeth down the toilet, not his real teeth! What are you like? How could you drop your real teeth down there? You'd have to dive in head first off the seat, probably with your mouth open.)

Mum always says it's a wonder Suki doesn't fall down the toilet, what with her tiny bottom.

Arrgh! Now I've thought about my sister's bottom.

Arrgh! Now I've thought about her on the toilet. I need to unthink it!

Then, of course, Raj told Mr James that his homework had fallen down the toilet, but that wasn't the same, because it didn't actually happen.

It was ... sort of ... a lie. Well, it was a lie. Well ... not a lie. An excuse, but not a true one.

2. I hadn't done stuff
   I should have done

I didn't fish Suki's strawberry lip gloss out of the toilet. I just flushed the loo, but it wouldn't go, so I bunged a lot of toilet roll on top of it.

Should I have fished it out? I didn't want to put my hand down the toilet.

Suki probably wouldn't want lip gloss on her

mouth after it had been down the toilet
(I wouldn't!). Although we kept Harry, and
he'd been down the loo.

But then nobody rubbed him on their
mouth afterwards.

3.   Someone had died

I knew Gran was OK because I saw her
over the park
with her
skateboard.
She'd been
practising
her kick flips
and ollies.

I hoped it wasn't Aunt Patsy who'd died.

I like her. She sends me two quid each

Christmas and she's got mad purple hair.

She's Mum's sister and she drives a lorry.

Serious Face

Mum had a Very Serious Face. What was up?

I tried to think of any other wrinkly old

relatives who might be on the way out.

Mum had a huge pile of paper in front of her with typing on it.

Harry was going mad in his cage trying to get to it. His little pink nose was pushed right out of his cage. It was big, thick paper and would have been a nice chewy dinner for him – or else something good to poo on.

'What have I done?'

'Nothing, Pig, you've not done anything wrong – well not that I know of – although the toilet is a bit bunged up. The thing is, Pig ... '

Mum took a huge breath and she wobbled a bit:

'... the thing is ... these are my divorce papers. I'm getting a divorce from your dad. I want you to be OK with it.'

I had that feeling you get when you eat a curry and you wake up in the middle of the night and it's sort of up in your throat. I felt sick.

'But he's my dad!'

Dad was a right laugh. OK, he couldn't paint stuff like Bob, or do Maths, or make rubbish pots.

He was always here, though (except when he wasn't). He didn't go out to work and he would always play football with me down the rec.

He used to let me eat just chips for tea and one day he forgot to get me up in the morning, so he let me stay off school and watch television all day with him.

Mum used to get a bit angry with him, but then

he'd make her laugh and dance around the kitchen with her.

He could burp the whole of 'God save the Queen' on one glass of coke.

He bought me a whoopee cushion and my plastic poo. The cushion doesn't work any more because Suki put a pin in it after I put it on her chair. (Her tiny bottom didn't really make it fart anyway.)

Mr Strange has taken the poo away from me at the moment.

Anyway, I was sure Dad would get fed up with

his bar on the beach and come home and probably buy me a new plastic poo and some new trainers before I grow out of my good ones.

Mum was spoiling it all. I felt myself getting really mad.

'Your dad will always be your dad, Pig, but you see, well, Bob and me ... '

And there it was! Bob, Bob, bobbing old Bob!

He was bobbing my dad right out of the house
and it was my dad's home! Not Bob's!

'No! No!'

And I was really
angry. I pushed all the
papers onto the floor.

'You can't do it! I won't let you!'

I ran out of the kitchen, slammed the door
and went into my room. I got the baseball bat
I had for my Unbirthday and smashed it into

the wall, just where Bob had painted a picture of me on a surfboard. Bits of the wall came off. Big bits. My painted face was all smashed.

I went to bed, but I didn't get to sleep right away. I could hear Mum and Bob talking in the kitchen.

How could they do this to Dad?

My dream

I had a dream. Mum and Bob were getting married in the chip shop. Mum was wearing her leathers and Bob was wearing one of his huge brown jumpers. Instead of a ring, I had the goldfish on a little whoopee cushion.

(In case you're worried, the fish looked OK and was moving a bit. You are soft!)

Anyway, I knew that as soon as I gave them the goldfish, they would be married.

Just as I gave Mum the goldfish, my dad flew into the shop. He swooped through the door. He was wearing a superman costume. He picked Mum up and flew away with her. (You really would have to be Superman to pick her up!)

Bob just started eating the fish and chips.

I asked:

    'Will Dad come back for me?'

and Bob said:

    'No!'

and he started stuffing fish and chips into MY mouth so fast I couldn't breathe.

When I woke up, I was trying to eat the duvet.

It was Monday morning and I got into my uniform without having a wash, so I wouldn't see Mum.

Monday morning Maths

Mum was in the kitchen and I didn't want to go in there, so I dashed out of the front door. I left my Maths homework and the ingredients for pineapple upside-down cake on the kitchen table.

(Harry dragged the Maths homework into his cage and ate most of it. He put the rest of it in his toilet.

I don't think the homework was right anyway. It was algebra and I just don't get it. Mum says you have to turn it all into fruit, but that doesn't help.)

(Judging by all the Maths Harry has eaten, I reckon he's better at Maths than I am. Maybe I'd learn more if I ate it.)

Mr Lamb, the new Maths teacher, was angry with us and he made everyone who hadn't done their homework stand up. He asked us where our homework was.

Blake couldn't do hers – she didn't even know what the date was to put at the top.

Frankie said he only had a solar-powered calculator and it was a cloudy day.

Saffron had one of those number padlocks on her locker and she had forgotten the number. But Sky said he could open those, so they went off together to get her homework out of the locker.

Raj said he had dropped his homework down our toilet.

I didn't say anything. I just looked at my feet. I wasn't going to tell everyone what had happened at home.

Mr Lamb made us stand at the front and told everyone to look at us. He said we would never get jobs if we didn't get good at Maths.

The great farmyard lesson

Mr Lamb's a nice teacher, even though Mum says:

> 'He looks about twelve.'

He lets us go up and do stuff on the whiteboard.

I like new, shiny teachers - they let you do stuff.

Our drama teacher is so old he looks like a tortoise and we have to make a lot of noise to keep him awake.

But how does Mr Lamb know what I am going to be like when I grow up? I might be an astronaut, or a judge on the X Factor, or a lion tamer. He didn't know!

Suddenly I hated him – really hated him.

So when Mr Lamb turned his back on us to write on the whiteboard, I went:

'Baaaa! Baaaa!'

Get it? Baa – lamb! It was just to wind him up. It was great. He turned round really quickly, but we were all sitting there, really quiet.

As soon as he turned his back:

'Baaaa!'

Then Zac started:

'Moooo! Moooo!'

Everyone was giggling and snorting. Even the girls joined in.

'Eee-aw! Eee-aw!'

Frankie did a really good horse's neigh. Blake wanted to join in, but she was laughing too much.

Mr Lamb had gone very red and was shouting at us.

'Be quiet! What's the matter with you? It's your own time you're wasting!'

By now we were all laughing and making noises to his face. Raj went:

'Quack! Quack!'

just as Miss Joseph walked in with Sky and Saffron. (They had broken Saff's locker – Sky had been kicking it.)

It all went very quiet. Really quiet. It was like all the noise was sucked out of the room by a noise-eating giant alien (we were doing similes in English again).

I could hear my heart beating in my ears. (Yes, I know where your heart is! You know what I mean!)

Then Raj said:

'Oh, poop!'

Miss Joseph sorts it out

If I thought Mr Lamb was angry, Miss Joseph was about twenty times as mad. There was steam coming out of her ears. Honest, I could see it!

'Rajesh Singh, who started this ... this ... farmyard?'

'It was all of us, miss!'

Good old Raj!

I could feel my hand going up. It was like one of those horror films where part of the body moves all by itself and the owner can't stop it.

I said:

'It was me, Miss.'

'Peter Ian
Green, I
should have
guessed!'

'I'm sorry, miss.'

I WAS sorry.

Sir looked really het up. His face was still red.

'Sorry isn't good enough, Peter. I want you

back here at the end of the day. You are going to teach the teachers a lesson and they are going to teach you a lesson.'

And she clicked out on her really high-heeled shoes. Clack, clack, clack! We could hear her all the way down the corridor. It was really quiet in there. Really quiet.

Teachers out of control

So after school I had to teach the teachers about fractions and they were out of control! (The teachers were out of control, not the fractions. Well, fractions always seem out of control, to me. Anyway, got to be clear.)

Mr Potter threw a Maths book and just missed Miss Reeves. It did stop Mr Strange trying to

cut her hair with a pair of school scissors,
though.

'Stop it! Stop it
now!'

I shouted at the top of my voice, but they just
carried on. I hated it. I didn't know what to
do.

I said to Miss Joseph:
'Help me. Please!'

Miss Joseph called out:
'Stop now! Staff meeting!'

All the teachers stopped straight away and went:

'Ohhh!'

and:

'Do we have to?'

Mr Strange said:

'That was really fun! Just like when I was at school!'

Then they all went out to the staff meeting.

Mr Strange says all they ever talk about is the toilets.

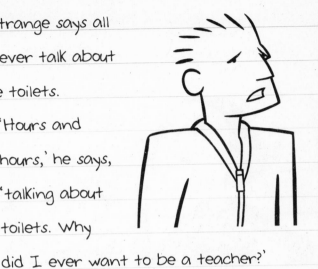

'Hours and hours,' he says, 'talking about toilets. Why did I ever want to be a teacher?'

To be fair, he isn't a real teacher. He does P.E.

Feelings

Miss Joseph looked at me.

'How was that, Peter?'

'It was rubbish!'

'It was rubbish for Mr Lamb, too. You've got to think about other people's feelings.

Mr Lamb is a person too. He's got a girl vampire baby. He's probably even got a mum. You have to think about others, Peter. I know just how you feel, Peter, because I think about it.'

I don't think she did know how I felt. I felt she should get her spiky shoe off my foot!

44

'He said that I would never get a job.'

'Maybe Mr Lamb didn't think enough about your feelings, Peter. Teachers are human, you know. Except, maybe, P.E. teachers. I think you would make a great teacher. You did well in front of the staff this afternoon.'

Then she said under her breath:

'They terrify me.'

I can always hear what grown ups say under their breath!

The way home

Miss Joseph phoned Mum and she came to get me from school.

We walked back up the hill. Mum was getting puffed out, so we sat down on the wall of the house of the bloke who has a big red car and doesn't like people sitting on his wall. We sat right on the sign that said:

'Do not ever sit on this wall!'

Mum's bottom didn't really fit at the back and it hung over the wall a bit, but she said:

'Gotta have a rest. It's a bloomin' long way.'

We talk about our feelings
(The soppy part)

We sat and didn't say anything for a bit.

I thought about what I had done to the wall

of my bedroom. I had spoiled everything.

'Sorry about the wall, Mum.'

'That's OK – Bob's plastered it. He'll paint

it again.'

That must have been a humungous plaster!

'Pig, I've been thinking. I won't get the divorce. I can see how upset you are.'

Then I could hear Miss Joseph's voice in my head. Are head teachers called 'head teachers' because they mess with your head?

'You've got to think about other people's feelings.'

I said:

'No, that's OK. Keep the Boring Old Bobster! I'll put up with him.'

'What made you change your mind?'

I said:

'Miss Joseph says I've gotta care about
how other people feel. Who knew?'

Mum said under her breath (but I heard her):

'Well, your real dad certainly didn't. Do you
know how I feel now?'

She whispered so I had to get really close.

I whispered:

'No.'

'Get closer.'

I whispered really quietly:

'How do you feel?'

'Like eating loads of chips!' she yelled in my

ear.

It was so loud that the Bloke with the Posh Car
came out and yelled at us:

'Can't you see the notice? Can't you see the

notice?'

Mum said:

'No, we're sitting on it!'

and we fell about laughing and ran up the rest
of the hill, with me towing Mum and then

50

running around to push her. We got in everyone's

way.

At the top of the hill Mum said to me:

'Now I've just got to tell Gran. That should

be easy ... '

I said:

'Ooo – I'd just send her a text!'

The next **PIG** book is

PIG's

Season's Finale

About the author

Barbara Catchpole was a teacher for thirty years and enjoyed every minute. She has three sons of her own who were always perfectly behaved and never gave her a second of worry.

Barbara also tells lies.